For Jasper

Published by Flying Eye Books, an imprint of Nobrow Ltd. 62 Great Eastern Street, London, EC2A 3QR.
Published in the US by Nobrow (US) Inc.
Printed in Belgium on FSC assured paper.

ISBN 978-1-909263-35-2

Order from www.flyingeyebooks.com

MR TWEED'S GOOD DEEDS

WRITTEN & ILLUSTRATED BY JIM STOTEN
FLYING EYE BOOKS

The sun was shining as Mr Tweed set out on his daily walk into town.
He strolled through the park and bumped into Little Colin Rocodile who wasn't looking very happy.

"I was flying my new kite when the string snapped and now I can't find it," he told Mr Tweed.

Mr Tweed decided to help Colin look for it. Can you help them find **1** lost kite, too?
Turn the page to explore the park.

"It feels good to help people," Mr Tweed thought to himself, as he left the park.
He was passing by some cottages when a voice stopped him in his tracks.

"Tibbles? Timkins? Where are you both?"

Oh no, Mrs Fluffycuddle's kittens have escaped and are hiding somewhere in the garden!
Can you help Mr Tweed and Mrs Fluffycuddle find **2** kittens over the page?

Having helped Mrs Fluffycuddle, Mr Tweed popped into the library on his way into town.
Inside the library, Mr McMeow was peering under the bookshelves.

"Good Morning, Mr Tweed. I'm afraid my pet mice
managed to escape while I was looking at books," said Mr McMeow.

A library is no place for **3** lost mice. Can you help find them? Turn the page to have a good search.

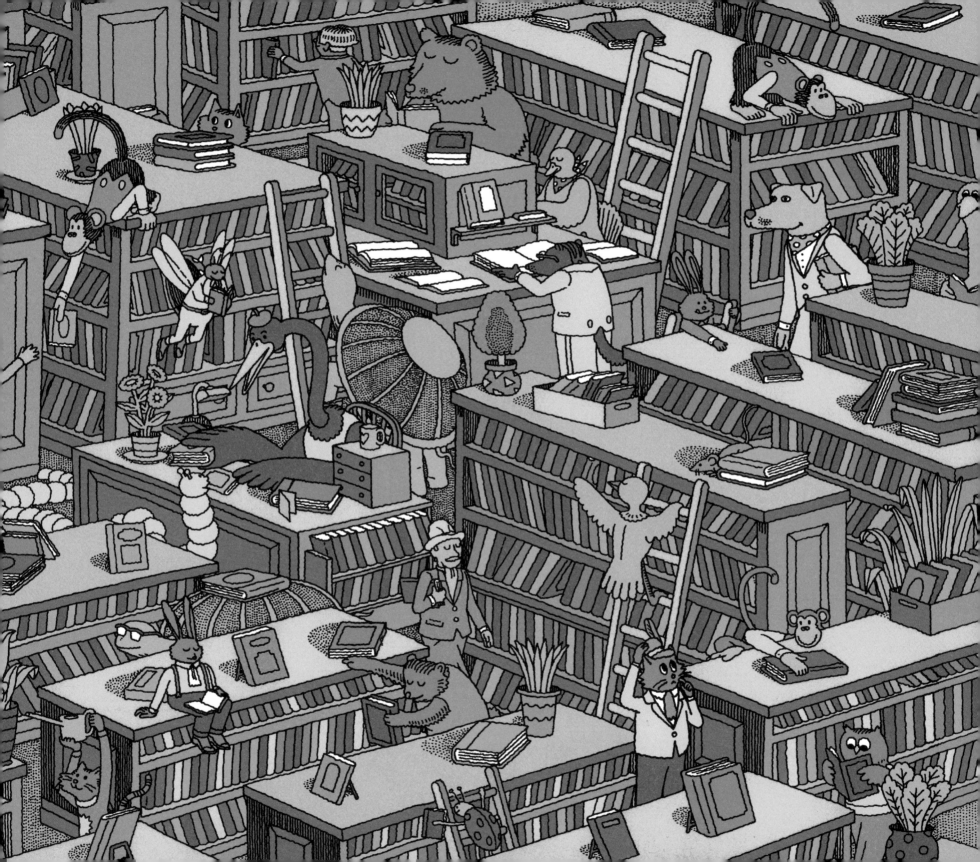

With a spring in his step, Mr Tweed left the library and reached the swimming pool.
Professor Ribbet was standing by the pool looking upset.

"You look like you need some help!" exclaimed Mr Tweed.

Oh dear, oh dear! Professor Ribbet's goldfish have jumped into the pool. It may not be as big as the sea,
but it certainly is full. Turn the page and see if you can find **4** goldfish splashing around.

Mr Tweed made his way through the woods, feeling very happy to have helped so many people already. But what was this? Big Bear Bob was looking for something in the treetops.

"Oh, hello, Mr Tweed," said Bob. "I was practising with my bow and I've lost all my arrows."

5 arrows in the woods won't be easy to find, can you help Mr Tweed look for them?

Mr Tweed emerged from the woods and into a field where the market was being held.
As he wandered through the market he noticed Herman Chimps frantically looking for something.

"Good day, Mr Tweed. I had a box of pineapples but I can't find them anywhere,
they must have rolled away!"

Where could **6** pineapples possibly be? Turn the page and see if you can spot them in the busy crowds.

Wandering out of the market and towards to the river, Mr Tweed
saw Little Penny Paws crying on the bridge.

"Oh, Mr Tweed, I was carrying a bunch of flowers that I'd picked for my mum, but the
wind caught them and they all flew into the river," she sobbed.

Can you turn the page and see if you can spot **7** floating flowers?

Mr Tweed couldn't remember a day when he had helped so many people! He ambled cheerfully into the busy town, only to bump into Billy Webber, looking a little bewildered.

"Hello, Mr Tweed. I had some socks hanging on my washing line and they have all blown away somewhere."

Socks can't go very far without a good pair of shoes... Turn the page and see if you can find **8** socks.

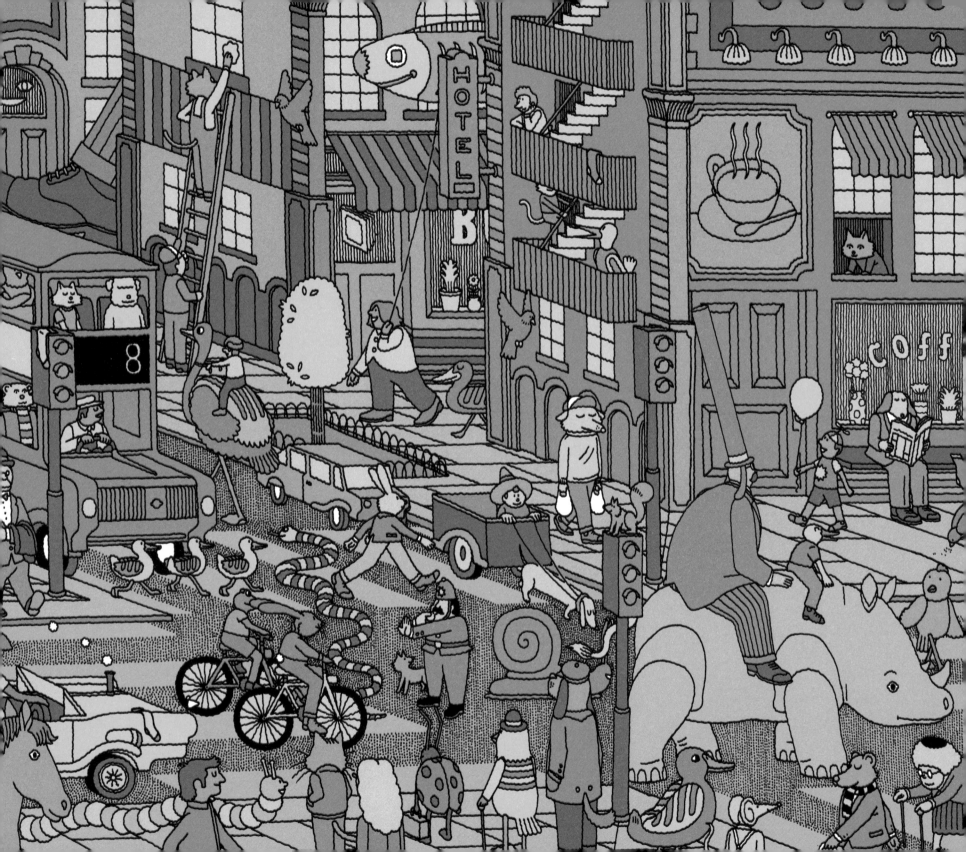

As Mr Tweed turned the corner, he saw the fair was in town and
Pingle Penguin came running towards him.

"Hello, Mr Tweed.
I won a bunch of balloons and let them go by mistake and now I don't know where they are!"

The fair is filled with Ferris wheels and rollercoasters, but can you help find **9** balloons over the page?

Mr Tweed decided it was time to head home.

Suddenly, Pete Weasel came running up and invited him around the corner. There was a huge street party and all the people that Mr Tweed had helped on his walk were clapping and cheering.

"We have thrown you a party to say thank you for all your help!" called Pete.

After a day of doing such good deeds, doesn't Mr Tweed deserve some nice gifts?
Hidden in the party scene on the next page are **10** presents. Can you help collect them all?

"Goodbye, Mr Tweed," everyone called.